Spooky Shipwreck

Look out for more
mermaid adventures:
Pirate Trouble
Treasure Hunt
Whale Rescue

Mermaid Rock

Spooky Shipwreck

Kelly McKain
illustrated by Cecilia Johansson

■SCHOLASTIC

A Sophie, un fuerte abrazo

Scholastic Children's Books,
Euston House, 24 Eversholt Street
London NW1 1DB, UK
a division of Scholastic Ltd
London ~ New York ~ Toronto ~ Sydney ~ Auckland
Mexico City ~ New Delhi ~ Hong Kong

First published by Scholastic Ltd, 2003
This edition published by Scholastic Ltd, 2006

Text copyright © Kelly McKain, 2003
Illustrations copyright © Cecilia Johansson, 2003

10 digit ISBN 0 439 95109 7
13 digit ISBN 978 0439 951098

Printed and bound by Tien Wah Press Pte. Ltd, Singapore

10 9 8 7 6 5 4 3 2 1

Papers used by Scholastic Children's Books are made from
wood grown in sustainable forests.

☆ Chapter One ☆

"Ouch!" cried Spirulina. "Stop it!"

All was not well on Mermaid Rock. Shelle
was trying to comb the seaweed out of
Spirulina's tangled curls – without success.
"Sit still!" she snapped, tugging at a knot.
"Mermaids must be neat and tidy."

"Being neat and tidy is a waste of time," Spirulina grumbled. "I could be off having adventures, you know!"

Coralie frowned at her. "Don't be silly," she said. "Mermaids are *far* too delicate for that."

Spirulina was about to argue, when she spotted a torn page of newspaper floating towards them. She fished it out of the water and held it up.

"Shipwreck found at Mermaid Rock!" she read. "What a perfect adventure for me!"

"You!" scoffed Shelle. "You'd be far too scared to swim about inside a shipwreck."

"Scared? I'm not scared of anything," declared Spirulina.

Just then, another scrap of paper washed up on to Mermaid Rock. Coralie scooped it up.

"So, you're not scared of anything?" she asked slyly.

"Nothing," said Spirulina firmly.

Coralie put the two pieces of newspaper together. "Not even ghosts?"

Haunted
Shipwreck
found at
mermaid Rock

"Of c-c-course I'm not scared of g-g-ghosts," said Spirulina, shivering.

In fact, Spirulina was *terrified* of ghosts. But she'd never admit it.

"Okay then," said Shelle, "we dare you to swim down to that haunted shipwreck."

"And bring back something pretty to prove you've done it," added Coralie.

"All right," said Spirulina. "I'll go this minute."

"Good," said Coralie.

"Bye," said Shelle.

And they went back to combing their hair and singing.

"Huh! They don't believe I'll do it," huffed Spirulina. "I'll show them!"

With shaking fingers, she strapped on her tool belt.

Then she dived off Mermaid Rock and began to swim.

As Spirulina swam further and further out to sea, the water got deeper and darker and colder.

Something loomed ahead in the darkness.

She switched on her torch…

…and there was the shipwreck!
It was ENORMOUS!

Trembling, Spirulina swam along beside
the shipwreck
until she found
a porthole. Then
she crossed her
fingers for luck and
slipped through.

What a sight! Inside the shipwreck all the metal was rusty and all the wood was rotten. Spirulina felt her way through the gloom.

Remembering her promise to Coralie, she started searching for something pretty to take back with her.

Suddenly there was a loud CLUNK! Spirulina spun around. Shadows skulked in the corner of the galley.

"Oh no," she gasped. "It's the g-g-ghosts of the shipwreck – they're c-c-coming to scare me away!"

She shuddered with fear
as the shadows came
closer…

And closer…

☆Chapter Two☆

Just in time, Spirulina turned off her torch
and darted between two broken planks.
She found herself in the captain's cabin.
Peering back through the gap, she saw
that the shadows weren't ghosts at all.
They were divers!

Dizzy with relief, she watched the two men picking things up and putting them into plastic bags. They took bits of rusty metal, twisted knives and broken pots. They even took rotten wood from the side of the ship. What *were* they up to?

Spirulina was suddenly startled by a noise behind her. It was a sniffly, snuffly, sobbing sound.

She turned on her torch and lit up a ball of soggy fur.

"Hello," said Spirulina softly. "I'm Spirulina. Who are you?"

Two frightened eyes stared back at her. "I'm Sparky, the ship's cat."

"What's wrong, Sparky?" Spirulina asked. "Why are you so sad?"

"It's those divers," Sparky wailed. "They're taking the ship apart! I'll soon be homeless!"

Spirulina and Sparky watched the divers putting more and more things into plastic bags. Every time they took something, Sparky sobbed even harder.

"There, there, don't cry," Spirulina whispered. She tried to give the little cat a cuddle – but she got a terrible shock. Her arm went straight through him!

"Aarghhh!" she screamed. "You're a g-g-ghost!"

Sparky burst into tears again. "Oh, please don't leave me," he howled. "I can't help being a … a … a you-know-what. You're my only friend. Except for the other ghosts, of course."

Spirulina went pale. "Other ghosts?" she gasped. "What other ghosts?"

Just then, two gloomy figures came floating through the wall. They were the ghosts of the captain and the cook. Spirulina screamed.

"It's another sneaky diver!" roared the ghost captain.

"Let's give her a jolly good haunting!" hissed the ghost cook.

"Oh, no!" cried Sparky. "Please don't haunt her! She's not a diver! She's a mermaid. She's my friend."

The ghosts stared hard at Spirulina, then smiled.

"Forgive us!" said the ghost cook. "Any friend of Sparky's is a friend of ours."

Spirulina stopped shaking and started smiling too. "Thank you," she said.

"Those divers are trouble," grumbled the ghost captain. "They're stealing all our things to put in a museum. If they carry on like this, there won't be anything left to haunt!"

"How awful!" cried Spirulina. "But why don't you just scare them away?"

"We've tried that already," said the ghost captain glumly. "It didn't work."

"You can't just give up," Spirulina insisted. "Have another go!"

"Well, all right," said the ghost captain.

Spirulina and Sparky watched as the two ghosts floated up to the divers.

The ghost captain rolled his eyes, moaning and groaning. But the divers were so busy working, they hardly noticed.

The ghost cook wailed and waved his arms. But the divers didn't even blink.

Both ghosts pulled off their heads, threw them in the air and danced a jig.

"Well, if *that* doesn't work, nothing will," Spirulina gasped.

It didn't work.

The ghosts put their heads on again and floated back into the hiding place.

"They weren't scared at all!" sighed the ghost captain sadly.

"They've won," grumbled the ghost cook grouchily.

"No, they jolly well have not," meowed Sparky. "Spirulina's right. We mustn't give up!" With that, he leaped through the gap.

Claws flying, he hissed and spat and screeched, right in front of the divers' faces.

But the divers kept working.

One picked up a
small toy and put
it into a plastic bag.

"Mouse!" cried
Sparky, leaping into
the bag after it.

"Oh, no!" groaned the ghost captain.
"That's his favourite toy!"

"Sparky, come back here!" called
Spirulina.

But Sparky stayed where he was. "No," he said firmly. "If Mouse goes, then I go too."

"We've got to save him!" cried the ghost cook. "But how?"

Just then a shoal of fish swam through the shipwreck, right in front of them. Seeing the fish gave Spirulina a good idea.

"Don't worry," she told the ghosts. "I've worked out how to save Sparky *and* scare the divers away."

The ghosts looked hopeful. "How?" they asked.

"I'm going to make a fish," she explained. "Well, half a fish, anyway. Half a *big* fish."

"I don't understand how making half a big fish will save Sparky," said the ghost captain, "but  we'll help you in any way we can."

"Good," said Spirulina. "Do you have any knives and forks?"

"Yes, but they're all broken and twisted," said the ghost cook, frowning.

"Perfect. That's exactly how I want them," Spirulina assured him. "I'll need a big piece of rusty metal too, and a nice chunk of rotten wood."

"Certainly," said the ghost captain, floating off. A few minutes later the ghosts returned with the things Spirulina needed.

Then she got to work, hammering and chiselling and sawing away with her tools.

Soon she had a disguise that was very rotten and very rusty but also VERY SCARY INDEED.

"That's amazing!" gasped the ghosts. "But what are you going to do with it?"

Before Spirulina could explain, they heard a huge ME-YOWL.

The ghost captain hurried over to the spy-hole. "The divers have filled all their plastic bags," he bellowed. "They're heading back up – and Sparky's going with them! Hurry, Spirulina!"

Spirulina crossed her fingers for luck. "By Neptune, I hope this works," she whispered. Then she put on her disguise and swam towards the divers.

☆ Chapter Three ☆

"I am Chompfish!" shouted Spirulina. The disguise made her voice sound deep and loud.

The divers leaped backwards and clung together in fright.

"What are you doing with these things?" roared Chompfish. "Are you stealing them?"

The divers shook
their heads.
Their knees
were trembling
inside their wetsuits.

"I don't believe you," bellowed
Chompfish. "I think you *were* stealing them.
And besides, I'm hungry. All I had for my
lunch was one skinny mermaid and two
tough old ghosts. That's not enough for a
growing chompfish like me!"

The divers'
eyes grew
wide
with fear.

Inside the disguise, Spirulina heaved at Chompfish's jaw. It crashed up and down hungrily. The twisted knives and forks flashed in Chompfish's mouth, looking just like terrible teeth. "Divers are my favourite pudding," she boomed.

The divers looked at one another. They did not want to be dessert. They dropped their plastic bags and swam away as fast as their flippers could carry them.

"And don't come back!" shouted Chompfish, although there was no danger of that.

As the ghost captain helped Spirulina to pull off the chompfish disguise, the ghost cook opened the bag and Sparky and Mouse were free!

"You did it, Spirulina!" cried the ghosts. "We all did it," giggled Spirulina, glowing with happiness.

"You've done so much for us," the ghost captain told her. "Is there anything we can do for you?"

Spirulina thought for a moment.

Then she smiled a very cheeky smile. She whispered something into the ghost captain's ear.

"Very well," he said, nodding.

After a long swim home, Spirulina pulled herself up on to Mermaid Rock. As ever, her sisters were sitting still, looking pretty and singing their favourite song. But they soon fell silent when they saw her.

"What did you bring me, then?" asked
Coralie. "A gold coin? A silver goblet?"
"Nothing like that," said Spirulina,
shrugging.

"Ha! We knew you wouldn't swim down
to that haunted shipwreck," sneered Shelle.

"Oh, but I did," Spirulina insisted. "And I brought something back to prove it. Something better than a gold coin." With that, she gave a long, low whistle.

The ghost captain, the ghost cook and Sparky rose out of the sea...

...and floated straight up to Coralie and Shelle.

"Aaaarrgghhh!" screamed Shelle, leaping into the air.

"Eeeeekk!" cried Coralie.

Their carefully combed hair stood on end with fright. "Okay! Okay! We believe you!"

Spirulina couldn't
help giggling,
just a little bit.

Once her sisters had calmed down
Spirulina introduced them to her new
friends. The ghost captain told them how
Spirulina had saved Sparky and scared the
divers away.

"And she taught us not to give up," added
the ghost cook.

"Gosh, Spirulina, you're so clever," cried Coralie.

"And brave too," added Shelle, smiling.

Then the ghosts gave Spirulina's sisters a display of haunting, and in return Coralie and Shelle sang them a mermaid song. As for Spirulina, she just stared far out to sea, daydreaming of new adventures.